Lili Chartrand · Illustrations by Rogé
Translated by Susan Ouriou

Taming Horrible Harry

Tundra Books

Published in Canada by Tundra Books,
75 Sherbourne Street, Toronto, Ontario M5A 2P9

Published in the United States by Tundra Books of Northern New York,
P.O. Box 1030, Plattsburgh, New York 12901

Library of Congress Control Number: 2005906930

Library and Archives Canada Cataloguing in Publication

Chartrand, Lili
[Gros monstre qui aimait trop lire. English]
Taming horrible Harry / Lili Chartrand ; Rogé, illustrator ; Susan Ouriou, translator.

Translation of: Le gros monstre qui aimait trop lire.
ISBN 10: 0-88776-772-9
ISBN 13: 978-0-88776-772-2

I. Rogé, 1972-   II. Ouriou, Susan III. Title.

PS8555.H43053G7613 2006   jC843'.6   C2005-904776-3

We acknowledge the financial support of the Government of Canada through the Book Publishing Industry Development Program and that of the Government of Ontario through the Ontario Media Development Corporation's Ontario Book Initiative. We further acknowledge the support of the Canada Council for the Arts and the Ontario Arts Council for our publishing program.

ONTARIO ARTS COUNCIL
CONSEIL DES ARTS DE L'ONTARIO

Printed and bound in China

1 2 3 4 5 6   11 10 09 08 07 06

For Béatrice, Lili
For Marilou, Uncle Rogé
For Meghan, Susan

Horrible Harry was a big, dirty, mean monster. He was, in a word, horrible. Now, Horrible Harry lived in a great forest where humans liked to wander. Horrible Harry's job was to scare them away with his terrible roar. He enjoyed his work. Hidden behind an old oak tree, he laughed himself silly every time he made a human skedaddle out of the forest.

One afternoon, Horrible Harry sat behind his oak tree as bored as he could be. He hadn't had a single visitor since morning. But then he spied a little girl. She chose a spot on a rock nearby, sat down, and pulled a book out of her bag.

Horrible Harry got to work. He let out a cry so awful that every single bird flew away. But the little girl, caught up in her story, sat bent over her book. Horrible Harry was confused. Then he was furious. He took a deep breath and let out the most bloodcurdling cry he knew!

The little girl dropped her book and ran off as fast as her legs could carry her.

Horrible Harry burst out laughing. He was mighty proud of that roar, his loudest ever. Maybe the wolf he'd eaten for breakfast had given him an extra boost. He looked around to make sure no one else was coming and scurried over to have a look at the book. Never before had he had to bellow *twice* to scare away an intruder. Could this thing be magical in some way? He picked it up. He sniffed it. He licked it and screwed up his face. It had no taste at all.

Horrible Harry hurled the book to the ground. It landed open at a gorgeous picture. Curious, he picked it up again and slowly turned the pages. The pictures were all so beautiful that he carried it back with him to his cave.

Dolores del Dragon was passing by Horrible Harry's cave when she noticed a light on. She peered inside. "What are you doing?" she asked. "Shouldn't you be keeping watch over the forest?"

"Uh . . . I found this, and I just can't put it down," said Horrible Harry. He held it out to Dolores.

"What a beautiful book! I know the story too, and it's wonderful!"

"A book?"

"Oh, Horrible Harry, don't you know what a book is?" The old dragon lady sighed.

So Dolores del Dragon explained that the little black marks next to the pictures in the book were letters. The letters formed words, then sentences, then a story.

"I want to know what it says!" said Horrible Harry.

Dolores del Dragon had a thought. "Horrible Harry, would you like to learn to read?"

Of all the creatures in the forest, Dolores del Dragon was the only one who knew how to read. All the others spent their time eating, sleeping, and terrorizing people who only wanted to spend a nice quiet day in the woods.

And so, Horrible Harry's lessons began. Every morning, he went to Dolores's place to learn his alphabet. He was so eager to understand the story in his book that it took him no time at all to learn how to read.

From then on, Harry did
nothing but read. Hidden
behind his old oak tree,
he gave up bellowing at the
humans who ventured into
the forest. He was too busy
reading his book. He read it
over and over and over again.

One morning, Harry was called before the Grand Council of Monsters and its leader, Mel.

"You've been letting down the side, old boy! All kinds of people have been frolicking in the woods since you've learned to read. We don't want your sort in our Grand Council of Monsters!" Mel bared his teeth and Harry fled.

Dolores del Dragon imagined Harry at home in his cave, crying, so she decided to pay him a visit. "Yoo-hoo! I've come to cheer you up," she called. But surprise, surprise! Harry was reading peacefully by the light of a small fire. "Well, well, Harry. I'm thrilled to see you reading!"

After that, Dolores del Dragon brought him more books: books she loved, and books she thought he would love. Each one was more wonderful than the last. Harry was as happy as he could be.

One evening, Two-headed Thomas
arrived at Harry's door, looking glum.
He saw Harry, all cozy with his book.
"Could you read me a story?" he asked,
hanging his two heads low.

"I'd love to!" said Harry, overjoyed at
seeing his friend again. He knew the story
in his book so well that he did a fantastic
job reading it out loud. Two-headed
Thomas returned home, his four eyes
bright with pleasure.

The next evening, Two-headed Thomas came back to the cave with Warty Monster in tow. "Read him the story I loved so much," he said to Harry.

Three pairs of eyes stared at Harry as he read. The next day, four. The day after that, twelve pairs of eyes were trained on him. Suddenly, a thirteenth pair appeared. It was Mel himself.

The other monsters were surprised, but no one dared to say a word. Mel was famous for his terrible temper tantrums.

In a corner of the cave, Dolores chuckled to herself. What had happened to the big, bad, horrible monsters that used to terrorize the whole forest? Now the old dragon could hear nothing but *oohs* and *aahs* of surprise.

Just then the sound of sniffling caught her attention. Mel was so touched by the story that he was blowing his nose into a big oak leaf.

Ever since that memorable day, all the monsters' heads have been so full of beautiful pictures and wonderful stories that they can't be bothered to do their jobs. Hidden deep in the forest, they don't feel like scaring away humans anymore. They're too busy daydreaming about beautiful princesses and the brave monsters that come to rescue them. *Oops*, sorry – and the brave knights that come to rescue them.

As for Harry, now that he's discovered how fabulous books are, he spends his days reading in his hiding place behind the old oak tree. He's the only monster who still keeps his eyes peeled for visitors, but not to scare them away. His fondest wish is to see the little girl again someday.

And that's why when he's finished reading for the day, Harry sets the little girl's book right where he found it. On top of it he places a rock shaped like a heart. Just in case.

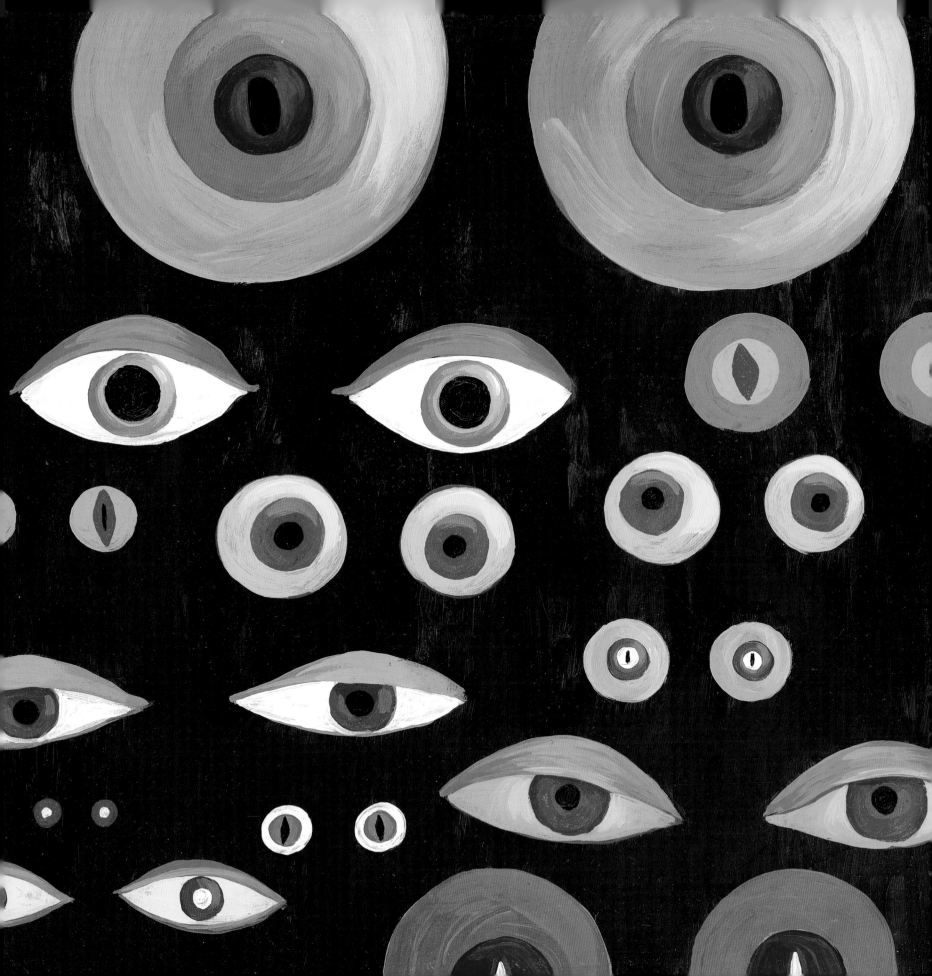